hell Mary

Book One: Full of Wrath

b y: Drayton W Jones

This series is dedicated to three important people. First, to my mom and my sister who show me superior examples of strong womanhood. Then, to my step-dad, who is the hardest worker I know. He always tells me to never go looking for a fight, but to always be ready for one. Family was the first institution. This story is for everyone who loves and fights for family.

The world fell because the world is fallen, and what is fallen is hell. Not far enough into the future the world is nearing death. Primitive measures of survival are now prioritized as the comforts of technology and globalization are a haunting memory. Mary sojourns here on this dying earth, praying and striving to survive just long enough. This is hell Mary.

I

Somewhere a white dove sat on a tree branch, covered in sunlight. Not in Hell. The sky was a deep purple there. It spread across the white brick city on the hill. No building was much taller than any other. Dried palm tree trunks lightly bent against the gusts of wind coming up from the dark sands. The sun said it's last goodbyes for the day and slipped beneath the horizon as the now dark sky blended with the ever-dark earth. Mary shifted slightly on her stomach causing a thud as the metal roof of the car popped up. She was small, barely 5'4", lean, with chopped dark haired. Her eyes were large and full of green. She had ten ear piercings in total and tattoos marked her dark tan skin on her right cheek and left arm. She wore green army pants, boots, and an old Nirvana t-shirt. Mary lay on top of a white 1957 Ford Fairlane with a 352 Thunderbird V8 engine. Tire chains covered all four tires and each were rusted in place. The wind pushed her short hair over the top of her head and down the left side of her face. She peered through the red dot sights on her M4. The large two storied building looked clear. *No Pirates, Darkfaces, or Crazies,* she thought.

Her head lifted as she lay her rifle next to her and pushed up with her arms to sit on the car roof. Six barked twice from the passenger seat beneath her, sticking his brown and black haired head out of the side window.

"Hush Six!" Mary whispered. The dog obeyed and pulled his head back into the car. Mary reached into her left cargo pocket and pulled out a crumpled pack of Camel's with one left. She retrieved a lighter from a small bag at her side. "Ya know Six, this is the last smoke I got but it doesn't matter. Can't smoke anymore after tonight anyway right?" Six yawned with a sigh and stuck out his tongue, panting.

The moon was full and reflected off of every white brick building and cracked up road. Sand dunes had formed on some of the open streets. Dried strands of brown grass snapped and waved in the wind as each stood momentarily in cracks in the road before being snipped off and carried away with each new gust. Mary and her car remained in darkness, parked at the very edge of the city, where the buildings stop and the dark sand begins; the edge of Hell. She finished her cigarette, flicked it into the sand, and jumped off the roof of the car, slinging her rifle over her shoulder. After a soft whistle, Six jumped out of the passenger window and followed her into the city.

Mary walked slowly as she approached a wide street with the two-story building. She puller her rifle off of her shoulder and gripped the hand and fore grips positioning her finger a twitch away from the trigger. Her left hand released the grip for a moment to motion for Six to sit at the entrance of the building, which was covered by two rot-iron gates chained at the center. The left gate's bottom hinge had rusted off and allowed the gate to be pulled forward from the bottom. Mary did so and crawled through the open space on the other side. Six tilted his head as he stared through the iron bars at his master. He stuck out his tongue and panted softly. Mary put her left finger up to her lips and Six sat by the gate obediently. Alone she stood in a marble courtyard. Much of the marble was cracked and there were several rows of large columns holding up a now caved in roof. On the opposite wall was a mural of some now forgotten war lord peppered with many bullet holes. *Lived in Havana my whole life and not once have I been in here,* Mary thought.

A sign hung above a large door across the courtyard which read *Abortion and Insemination Clinic*. Mary shuddered and then inhaled deeply as she walked towards the door then, thrusting her leg forward, she kicked it open; she splintered the wood at the hinges. Through the new opening was a dark hallway, illuminated only momentarily by the flickering florescent lights which dangled by tangles of cords from the ceiling. A slight buzz from the flickering lights masked all the other sounds that could be in the hall. Mary tread slowly, rifle in hand, casting a dark flickering silhouette against the cream colored walls. Flashes of smeared blood, forceps, brass shells, and what looked like skin appeared on the floor with each spasm of light that was briefly cast down. A crumpled and half rolled up poster lay on the floor among the abandoned metal instruments and bits of human—infant and adult. Mary stepped on the bottom corner of the poster and pressed her other boot near the rolled half, sliding her foot up until the poster was flat. She flicked on the small light that was fastened next to the rifle's barrel. Printed on the poster were the words:

Free abortions up through the 40th week of Pregnancy

Mary sighed and brushed the poster to the side with her foot. The hallway ended with an open doorway. Mary raised her rifle to guide the light into the pitch black; it was a windowless concrete room. Rows of metal shelving stood lined in rows, each containing what appeared to be glass tubes of red liquid. Her heart throbbed. She instinctively reached for her cargo pocket for a cigarette. *That's right, I just quit.* Her trigger finger quivered as it pointed straight forward. Her eyes tightened shut, then released open. A bead of sweat ran down her curved cheek and collected on her lips. She licked it before it fell to the floor. Mary rushed toward the third row. Each tube was labeled alphabetically; she knew where to go. *Castile.* The glass tube felt cold in her hand. Frantically she turned and strode over to a set of drawers and tore them open. One slid off of its rails and onto the floor, bursting apart. Syringes rolled a thousand directions across the dark cold floor. Mary grabbed the first one her fingers touched and slid the glass tube into the top opening. She pulled a needle out from her shirt and fastened it to the end of the syringe. Popping the light off of her rifle, she held it in her mouth as she peered down and lifted her shirt. *I have to do this now.* She thrust the needle into her lower abdomen and syringed the red liquid until the tube was empty.

"FUCK!" The light fell from her mouth as Mary pulled the needle out and dropped the tube onto the floor. She inhaled deeply several times and wiped sweat off of her face. Mary turned her head suddenly toward the doorway as she heard Six howl. Six only howls at two things. Other dogs…and Darkfaces. Mary gripped her rifle and fastened the light back into place as she sprinted out of the room and down the flickering hall, jumping over the pieces of wood from the kicked in door. She abruptly stopped once she stepped back out into the cool night of the courtyard. A soft blue glow was held by the marble as the moon peeked through the clouds.

"**Why are you in our city**?" a muffled robotic-like voice spoke but Mary could not see it's owner. She did not respond, but pulled her rifle up to her shoulder, peering through the sights. "**Havana is a dark zone**." There was still no sign of the disfigured voice's owner, or if it was alone.

"Six," Mary whispered. "**We have your dog**." Five tall figures dressed in black leather stepped out from behind several of the pillars. Each of their faces were covered in a sort of black material. Each wielded an AK-47 with a bayonet. "**Did you take some of the children?**" the one in the middle of the group spoke as he stepped forward. He slung his rifle over his shoulder and pointed at the kicked in doorway behind Mary, cocking his head to the side. "**Those children are to be raised as slaves. We will use them to save the world. You are a thief and a trespasser; you will come with us. Drop your weapon, NOW**."

"Hey fuck face, CATCH!" Mary threw her rifle at the dark figure in the center of the group and reached behind her, pulling out a Glock 17 from her back holster. *CRACK! CRACK!* Mary fired two shots at the two men to the left of the leader, snapping each of their heads back as the lead cut through their faces. Red splattered on the columns behind them. Mary dove behind a marble pillar. The two to the right of the leader raised their rifles and squeezed their triggers in unison, zipping .30 caliber bullets through the night, shattering bits and chunks of marble. The firing stopped and the sound of metal clinking across the ground grew closer as Mary saw a grenade roll past the column where she took refuge. She sprang up and leapt away as the explosion shot her even further through the air. Marble dust and bits rained down into the rubble of the courtyard. The three men shouted at each other. Mary's head felt heavy. Her vision blurred. She could barely make out the three silhouettes in the smoke. Suddenly, three flashes of light shot through the dust with a booming noise and each silhouette dropped with a thud to the marble floor. A new figure emerged from the dust. A tall man in boots, cargo pants and a tattered Levis jacket bent down, and holstered his Desert Eagle. His thick, rough hands gently lifted Mary's head and just before everything went black she heard him say, "My name is Jim, I'm going to help you, we have to leave now." *A saint*, she thought.

II

The Ford Fairlane crept slowly across the sand as it approached a large cage-like structure of bones and what looked like wax boulders at the base. Each bone was nearly twenty feet in height stretching up to the midnight blue sky littered with stars before curving at the ends back toward each other. The wind swept across the dunes of the dark sand with a slight howl, making it and the sound of the V8 engine the only audible noise in Hell.

Mary felt something warm, coarse, and wet rub across her cheek and up over her eye. She felt it again. Mary peeled her eyes open and sat up quickly. Six barked suddenly and panted, half climbing into her lap. Mary swiveled her head around sharply looking for her gun. Jim caught her eyes in the rearview mirror.

"Good, you're awake," he almost whispered. Mary saw her M4 propped up in the front seat. She shot her arm forward, grasping the fore grip. "Easy," Jim said coolly. He had already un-holstered his pistol and had the barrel pointed at her temple. "I'm gonna pull over here and then you can drive when I'm sure your head's good, alright?" Jim holstered his gun and quickly pressed on the brakes and shut off the ignition. Opening the driver's door Jim stood and walked over toward one of the large bones and propped against it with one hand and rested the other on his hip. Mary noticed red splatters across his jean jacket and his hands. Six crawled his front half across Mary and poked his head out of the window and waged his tail.

"You like him, huh?" Mary whispered in his ear and she pet his neck with both of her hands. "We'll see." She opened the door to let Six jump out and then retrieved the keys and her rifle before slowly walking over to Jim.

"So I guess you saved us huh?"

"Right place, right time I guess." Jim turned around and reached into his front jacket pocket for a cigarette. He raised his eyebrows toward Mary.

"I quit." she shook her head as she spoke. Jim shrugged his shoulders and retrieved his lighter.

"So why were you in Havana?" she asked.

"Real question is why were *you*?" Jim spoke as his cigarette bobbed up and down between his lips. He drew in a long drag and blew out the white smoke into the night air. You have a nice car. V8. Full tank, two weapons, a good dog," Six kept wagging his tail as he stood by Mary. "And a million reasons I'm sure to be nowhere near hell."

"There was something there I needed."

"*That bad?*"

"Yes. Something I can't live without."

"Well…" Jim paused and lifted his eyebrows again toward Mary.

"My name is Mary."

"Well Mary. We should camp out here. It's relatively safe. Haven't seen any Crazies for three weeks. Only a few Pirate ships here and there. We'll build a small fire, cook some dinner, and then you can tell me what it is you can't live without." Six panted and barked with approval, nudging Mary in the hip with his head. She nodded.

"Ok. But I don't remember your name."

"Me neither." Jim said casually as he walked past Mary towards the car. He turned and pulled his jacket back on the right side and pointed to a patch sewn onto a mechanic's shirt.

"Jim." Mary said.

"First shirt I found after I escaped. Didn't remember my name, so I thought this was as good as any." Mary grinned.

"I hope you don't mind; I threw my bag in your trunk." Jim held out his hand. "Keys?"

III

A single cloud drifted across the dark sky temporarily hiding the moon from view. The other light came from the thousands of stars and the small fire below. Jim had begun to cook a small pot of beans over the fire as he had suggested and Six had turned around three times in the sand and then lay down, content in his new bed. Mary leaned against the driver's door of her car as she checked her rifle's chamber and barrel for sand. Jim crouched down and dug in his bag, pulling out two small bowls.

"Where did you find an M4?" Jim raised his eyebrows as he dipped each bowl into the simmering pot.

"Guantanamo Bay." Mary grinned.

"No shit? Well that's as good a place as any." Jim handed a bowl to Mary. "Sorry, no spoons." Six cocked his head to the side as he watched the food passed across the fire. "Right, almost forgot." Jim reached in his bag and pulled out an unusually large bone and tossed it to Six. He caught it in his mouth and immediately began wagging his tail as he chewed on one of the ends. Mary's eyes pleaded for an explanation. "Tiger bone. It escaped from a zoo…" Her eyes widened. "It's a long story." Jim then reached inside his jacket. Mary instinctively released the bolt catch on her M4 and flipped the fire selector to auto with her thumb and lined the sights at Jim's head. Six reared up and barked. Jim immediately threw his hands up, dropping his bowl. "Holy Shit!"

"What were you reaching for?!" Mary maintained her aim.

"What?"

"Why did you reach into your jacket?" Mary's lips moved forcefully.

"I found some rum a few days back. Was gonna take a sip— look, you need to calm down."

"There is no calm—we're in Hell, remember."

"I'm sorry, you're right." Jim sighed. "Okay? *You're right.*" Jim said softly.

Mary slowly lowered her rifle.

"Look, you want some rum?" Jim grinned. She sat her rifle down in her lap and picked up her bowl.

"Sorry I made you drop your food. And no, I can't drink."

"What, are you knocked up or something?" Jim laughed as he talked. Mary just stared at him across the fire.

"Oh. Son of a bitch. You're pregnant."

"That's why I was in the clinic. In Havana. My dead husband's DNA was there. We promised we would have a family right before…before the world died. I promised. That's what I can't live without. *Our child.*" Mary spoke slowly and calmly. Jim stared at the fire before taking a slow sip of rum and then tossing the bottle over toward his bag.

"Look. I think you're fucking crazy." Jim rolled his eyes at himself as Mary shot him a look. "What I mean is…look, crazy was the wrong word." He quickly broke eye contact and stared at his spilt bowl of beans that has soaked into the dark sand.

"You're the crazy one." Mary grinned, stretching out her leg and poking Jim's boot with the tow of her boot. "Calling a pregnant woman *crazy*… that's playing with some fucking fire ya think?" He looked up, smiled, and then burst out a quick explosion of laughter. Six perked his head up, giving the large bone a quick respite.

"So where you headed?" Jim said, fighting laughter.

"Badlands." Mary replied quickly.

"Badlands? Like, the old Dakota states Badlands?! Holy shit. *Ho-ly Shit*!" Jim shook his head.

"It's nearly 3,000 miles away." Mary turned her head towards Six who stuck out his tongue and panted. "Holy Shit."

"Why? What's there?" Jim stared intently at her eyes.

"It's where my husband was from. He had said it was one of the few places in the world that hadn't fully died yet. There are still wild flowers. There are no rapists, or pirates, or gangs. Just people. Maybe even good ones."

"It sounds great." Jim sighed. "But I'll believe it when I see it."

"You think it isn't real?" Mary asked straightly.

"I don't know many things that are real anymore."

"What do you know?"

"I know that if you bleed enough, you die." Jim stared once more at the fire. It was starting to die. Mary reached over to pet Six's neck, but kept staring at Jim. His eyes glossed a bit.

"Well," Mary said, trying to sound cheerful, "do you know what the fuck this thing is here in the middle of Hell?" She nodded to the large pillars and wax like boulders behind Jim.

"Of course." Jim said, sitting up. "It's a whale carcass." Mary gasped a little.

"I didn't know any remains of the before-creatures were left."

"Most are gone. I've seen some before-creatures near the Mexican cliffs. I think the Dark-Face Lord keeps them as pets." Jim sighed. "Well, since you made me spill my food…"

"Yeah, sorry about that." Mary frowned.

"It's fine, but I'm gonna go see if I can scavenge something. I found an abandoned truck the other day. Maybe 3 miles west of here." The moment Jim stopped speaking, they heard a shrill scream, eerily close. Jim sprang up, unholstering one of his Desert Eagles. Mary flicked her safety selector to full auto as she vaulted to her feet.

"It seems to be just on the other side of the whale," she whispered.

"Ok." Jim said as he began motioning with his free hand. "I'll go around the tail, you advance up and come around the head. Hopefully there's no more than two."

"Two what?"

"Crazies."

Mary nodded and watched Jim disappear around the back side of the carcass. She turned and signaled for Six to follow at her side. Creeping towards the head of the whale, she pointed her rifle directly forward. **CRACK! CRACK!** Mary knew that sound. Desert Eagles made a distinct thud when they were fired. She turned and saw dull light flash twice through the rotting fat of the whale. "Six!" Mary whispered and motioned him to begin running with her. Mary reached the head of the whale and turned the corner. She almost yelled for Jim when something slammed into her stomach. She heard a small voice gasp. Mary fell and rolled over in the sand, facing a young, wide eyed girl with bright red hair. She couldn't have been more than twelve years old.

"Mary!" Jim yelled as he sprinted towards them. Suddenly, a mound of sand began to shift and pour off of a dark rising figure. As the sand fell, suddenly a large man stood just feet from Mary and the young girl, covered in black robes and a red cloth mask. He raised an AK-47 at the girl. Mary whistled for Six who grabbed the girl's collar in his mouth and began to drag her away.

CRACKKKKCRACKKK!! The dark figure missed his first several shots at the girl's head. Mary rolled to grab her rifle and fired two quick shots at the figure's knees. A fierce cracking noise was made when the 5.56 rounds ripped through his flesh and bone. He dropped to his knees and screamed. Mary recovered her aim and aligned the sights on his face.

"Wait!" Jim gasped as he caught his breath. We need the ammo." Mary slowly lowered her rifle and Jim flicked a karambit knife from his belt and sunk the blade into the man's throat, running it across from one side to the other. Red seeped through the fabric and splattered onto the sand as the man in black collapsed forward onto the ground. "Fuckin' crazies."

"You ok?" Mary asked.

"Never been better. Where's the girl?"

"Shit! Six! Come Six!" Mary shot up and the two ran back towards the car. They darted around the side of the whale and nearly ran into Six who barked twice the moment he saw Mary. Mary furrowed her brow. They heard the sound of an engine starting and tires spinning in the sand. The Ford Fairlane sped off into the distance.

"She stole my car!" Mary exclaimed.

"Well shit. She stole your car." Jim said, taking out another cigarette.

IV

Mary and Jim left dark footprints in the dark sand as they walked back toward Havana. Six stayed several yards out in front, sniffing the ground. Each grain of sand shimmered a little as it was overturn by their boots and briefly caught the light of the moon. Mary carried her M4 and Jim had taken the AK from the dead crazy.

"Do you think it was a setup?" Mary asked.

"I think she was just scared." Jim's cigarette bobbed up and down as he spoke. "Crazies don't keep children. They kill them, or worse. She was probably just trying to escape."

"How many hours of darkness do we have left?"

"Hmm." Jim looked up at the sky. "Maybe four."

"We can't be caught out here in the light. It exposes all of Hell. That's how people get caught." Mary sighed. A soft rumbling grew into a prominent noise.

"I know that sound." Jim suddenly stopped.

"It's a pirate ship!" Mary whispered. Jim nodded toward a small dune to their left. Six turned his head back to them and barked at Mary. The two sprinted across the sand as Six followed. Two lights shone against another sand dune further ahead and then turned to face them. The diesel engine grew louder. They sprinted faster, kicking up sand with furious steps. Suddenly Jim's feet sank and he disappeared into a hole.

"Jim!" Mary turned and saw the sand begin to disappear in front of her and she jumped to the side before the ground gave way. Six whimpered as he carefully stepped towards the edge of the hole and cocked his head to the side, looking down at Jim.

"I'm ok!" Jim coughed in the darkness. "I've seen these before. They're…"

"Slave-traps." Mary whispered to herself, staring at the tattoo on her arm. The diesel ship was upon them now. Mary looked up from the pit and stared straight ahead past the bright lights. Her and Six's silhouettes stood tall and black against the blinding brightness of the truck. It stopped just before the pit making a sharp high pitched noise as it braked. The ship was a large black semi-truck with tank treads where the wheels would normally be. It pulled a black yacht on a trailer with a large black flag. Seven men poured out of the truck and the boat. All were armed with M4s, Glocks, and AKs. They had boots and military pants and jackets. The two men in front, the apparent leaders, wore navy berets.

"Welllll Shit." The first man with the beret said as he shone his Glock with a mounted light into the pit. He had a thick beard and a scar over his left eye. "The female is the one that's supposed to fall in the trap, not this piece of …" The man studied Jim's face, "Tex-Mex trash." He spat into the pit as Jim stepped out of the way. The man glanced up as he wiped his beard. "Drop that M4 right now sweetie before I kill Tex here." Mary glanced down at Jim who shook his head. She tossed the rifle to the ground. "Now tell me something sweetie. You face fuck?" The other men began to laugh and grin. "Cause they pay extra for face fuckin." Mary reached behind for her 6o'clock holster and pulled out her Glock 17.

CRACK! CRACK! She hit the man in the face and the neck. Blood splattered on the men directly behind him and gushed from the left artery in his neck as he fell forward into the pit.

"You mean like that?" Mary said, taking aim at the other leader. Clicking noises mixed with shouts were heard as the other men moved their safety selectors to full auto and aimed at Mary's head. One of the grunts strode forward and grabbed what looked like a small crossbow that had been slung on his waist and shot it at Mary. The arrow nicked her shoulder and pierced her shirt, hooking onto the collar. The arrowhead was fastened to a wire and was suddenly yanked back by the man, ripping the shirt from her. The men resumed their laugher. Six jumped in front of Mary and growled at them, barring his teeth.

"That's called a no means yes hook" The grunt said laughing as he pulled the shirt back to him. As he reeled in the wire, it fell into the pit and stopped. He tugged on the wire twice. "Fuckin' piece of..." Suddenly the man disappeared into the pit as the wire pulled him in. ***CRACK!*** Bits of brain, bone, bloody hair, and flesh shot up out of the pit.

"ENOUGH!" Exclaimed the other pirate with the beret. He reached for a flash grenade on his belt, pulled the pin, and dropped it into the pit.

"Jim!" Mary screamed as she saw him cover himself with the half-headed grunt. Desert Eagle rounds will do that to a head. The leader then shot a Taser at Mary who collapsed onto the ground. Everything went dark as Six lay beside her.

Mary jolted forward. She was still shirtless, wearing a black bra and her camo pants. Her boots and socks had been taken. Her eyes focused and she quickly grabbed a blanket that she just noticed and draped it over herself. Seven other girls were in the room sitting against the opposite wall. Seven. The youngest looked about 13, while the oldest appeared around Mary's age. Some wore dirty old jumpsuits while others were simply in pants and bras as Mary was. The room was lit by a single bulb. It was dark and green and rusted.

"Where are we?" Mary asked hoarsely. Her mouth was very dry.

"The hull of the ship. Harrod's ship." Said the oldest. She had black hair and was wearing one of the dirty jumpsuits. She was pregnant.

"Who the fuck is Harrod?" Mary said as she spat out some dried blood.

"He's one of Captain Hyde's pirates. Capt. Hyde of the Blackship Pirates. Harrod, He…" She stopped speaking and took a few steps forward towards Mary and began to whisper. "He sells sex slaves to the Blackfaces and the Crazies."

"How do you know this?"

"I'm Harrod's wife. Elizabeth." KNOCK! KNOCK! Mary startled back from the door. It creaked open. The man in the navy beret stepped in. He had a dark goatee and wore sunglasses. *It's fuckin' dark in here*, thought Mary.

"You're turn," he said, looking at Mary.

Jim thrust himself forward, sitting up aggressively, nostrils flaring as he inhaled.

 "Calm down son, calm down!" An elderly man who had been sitting on the floor against the wall slowly stood. He had a large stick which worked as his cane. He was severely bent over, and looked nearly eighty. He wore a single grey robe. Jim was sitting on a thin blanket on a cold metal floor in a rusting metal room with a single light bulb dangling from a wire in the middle of the ceiling. Jim was shirtless and his boots had also been taken.

"*Where is SHE?!*" Jim snareld.

"Who? Who is she?" The old man's voice creaked as he spoke.

"We were captured by" Jim was interrupted by thc old man's soft voice.

"Yes, yes, by the Blackship Pirates. Your friend was probably taken to…" The man paused.

"Where?!" Jim pleaded.

"Down the hall." The man frowned and turned to sit back down.

"What's down the hall?" Jim stood.

"Harrod's harem. He sells sex slaves. Mostly to the Blackfaces, sometimes to the Crazies if they are willing to negotiate—and that's a big if." Jim strode towards the metal door. It had a single wheel in the center of it, like a submarine. The wheel wouldn't budge. Jim prided himself on his strong hands. Mechanic's hands. "It's locked unless the guard opens it to bring food."

"What's your name? Why are you here?" Jim asked as he sighed and walked back over to the man. Jim leaned against the wall and slid down next to him.

"My name is Zachariah." The man spoke softly. His eyes glossed a little. "I was just a drifter, like you. Now I'm kept here to work, when I can. I'm a good cook."

"I thought the Blackships only dealt in arms and cocaine. Sex slaves too?" Jim stared at the door as he spoke. His large muscles moving up and down slowly with each heavy breath.

"They did. My guess is that this Harrod, the captain of this ship, began running girls on the side."

AHHHGH! A loud scream shot down the hallway from the other side of the door. Jim shot up to his feet. "That's Mary!" Jim's breath's quickened. He jumped towards the door and began banging on it with his fists. "Where did you say that room was?"

"Down the hall, to the right. Door at the very end."

"Good. When they come. When they open the door. Knock the light with your cane." Jim stared at the man who nodded reassuringly back at him.

"HEY!" yelled a voice from the other side of the door. "SHUT THE FUCK UP!"

"Come in here and MAKE ME!" Jim yelled back. The wheel on the door turned. Jim nodded toward Zachariah who shattered the light bulb with his cane. It was now pitch black. A thin stream of light appeared when the door opened. A large man in military gear stepped in. Jim saw the knife on his belt. By the time the man had stepped into the room Jim had jumped on the man's back with his left arm wrapped tightly around his neck. *UGH!* The man spun wildly and slammed Jim against the walls several times. Jim's lungs struggled. His breath was gone. He reached blindly for the man's knife. He found the handle, removed it from its sheath and stabbed the man in the stomach. Once. Twice. Threefourfivesixseveneight times. He did it so fast that the blood was delayed in spurting out.

The man slowly dropped to his knees and Jim's feet now touched the floor as he stepped over the man's head, gripping his hair with his fist momentarily before shoving him down. Jim noticed the man's pistol and took it, shoving it into the waist of his pants. He stood momentarily in the doorway. A dark silhouette covered in blood, turning to the right.

<u>V</u>

"She was found driving a Ford Fairlane sir." A tall man with a moustache and a red beret had walked into a large cabin aboard the Black Phantom. The room had red carpet, with dark wooden walls and ceiling. It was dimly lit by Victorian style lamps on dark wood furniture. On the wall behind the Captain's desk was a large map of the Gulf of Mexico. Captain Hyde stood from his chair. His two Dalmatians stood as well. He was very large. Nearly 6'6", heavy, with a large grey beard. He wore a Navy jacket, cargo pants, and boots. His belt held a holstered Colt .45. He strode across the room. His two Dalmatians followed.

"Where is she?" His voice boomed.

"She is aboard Harrod's cruiser. He will be arriving here at the Phantom at 0500." The man stopped and sighed as if he were going to continue speaking.

"What is it Daniels?" Captain Hyde spoke firmly as he pet the top of one of the dog's heads. The other whimpered for attention. Hyde looked down at them. "Hush Nero! I am petting Marcus." He stepped closer to Daniels, inches from his face. "Just tell Harrod to *not* delay. I *MUST* see Elizabeth!"

Miles away, Harrod's cruiser sped along the dunes in the dark. The diesel engine hummed and the two bright headlights shone ahead, prompting sidewinders and rats to retreat to their holes and hideaways. *AGHH!* Jim sprinted down the dark green and brown rusted hallway as Mary's screams grew louder. His nostrils snarled. His teeth were clenched. His face set. He reached the cracked door at the end of the hall and kicked it open. Mary was handcuffed to a bed. There were five men in the room; Harrod stood behind the bed trying to restrain Mary's legs. One of the men kept trying to dodge Mary's kicks as he tried to pull off her pants; the other three men stood at attention by the door. Every head turned once the door swung open. Jim wasted no time pulling the pistol from his wasteband and shooting the man in the head who had been struggling at Mary's legs. Two men at the door grabbed Jim's arms and knocked the gun from his hand. Harrod began to crawl over the bed when Mary kicked him in the chest. He turned and punched her in the throat; she wheezed and gasped.

Jim pushed against the floor and slammed the two men against the wall, knocking him loose from their grip. He leapt over towards Harrod who was just stepping off of the bed. Jim punched him in the face, knocking him back against the wall. Before Harrod could regain his balance Jim punched him in the face again. *"LET HER GO!"* Jim spat and nearly frothed at the mouth as he spoke. Harrod looked up at Jim, blood dripping from his nose and lip. He grinned.

"Jim! Look out!" Mary screamed.

Jim started to turn then suddenly shook violently as he was Tasered to the floor. Three other men in dark military uniforms and AK-47s entered the room.

"Sir, we have arrived at the Phantom." Harrod slowly stood, wiping the blood from his lip.

"Bring them up to the deck." He spat on Mary and laughed, walking out of the room.

The Black Phantom was a large ship. Two dark green military trucks pulled an oversized trailer which held up a large black Navy cruiser. Captain Hyde stood on the deck by the wheel with two guards in red berets next to him. Twenty men lined the deck against the rails. It was nearly dawn. Pink and deep blue light lined the horizon. Harrod's cruiser pulled up next to the Phantom's deck. The heavy purr of the diesel engine shut off. Two thin, white haired men in grey jumpsuits lowered a metal bridge with chain railing for Harrod to cross. He gestured for his men to follow with Jim and Mary. One of the pirates squeezed Mary's ass as she stepped onto the bridge. Turning quickly, she kicked the man over the side of the rail and down into the sand. His neck had snapped; a permanent look of shock rested on his face as blood began to soak the sand.

"Contain the prisoners!" Harrod exclaimed, turning to his men and unholstering his pistol. He pointed it towards a frightened young pirate. "Understand?"

"Harrod, what prisoners are those?" Hyde shouted, his voice booming from the other ship.

"My Captain!" Harrod lifted his arms to Hyde as he turned and crossed the bridge. "I have saved your daughter Elizabeth from these drifters!"

"Harrod, my friend, bring her! Where is she?!"

"My men are retrieving her as we speak." Harrod turned back and glared at Jim, then grinned at Mary as he stared at her bra. "These two tried to buy Elizabeth from the Darkfaces."

"Bring them Immediately!" Captain Hyde's voice boomed. He gestured to his two lieutenants with his Colt .45. The two pirates dressed in navy camo jumped the railing on the deck and sprinted toward the the bridge and took Mary and Jim. Captain Hyde then motioned with his hand for his men to put them on their knees as he descended to the deck. The two pirates shoved them onto the deck floor and aimed their rifles at the back of their heads. Jim's head slammed against the hardwood first, but he extended his leg just in time to catch Mary's, breaking her fall. They both struggled to their knees. Hyde's black combat boots echoed across the deck as he walked towards them. "You," the Captain spoke aggressively towards Jim. "you tried to BUY my daughter?!" Captain Hyde jabbed Jim in the chest with the muzzle of his pistol. He raised the barrel, running it up Jim's chest and using it to pull up his jaw. Hyde knelt down and the two locked eyes. "Did you?"

"PA-PA!" A young girl, around twelve years old with bright red hair emerged from below deck aboard Harrods's ship. She began sprinting across the bridge. Harrod turned, wide eyed, glaring at his men. As she ran to her father she locked eyes with Mary and suddenly stopped.

"Elizabeth! Hyde exclaimed, wide-eyed. "Come! What is wrong? These people will not…"

"She saved me." The young girl then sprinted over towards Mary, embracing her neck. One of the pirates reached for the girl's arm.

"Stop!" Hyde barked at the lieutenant. "Elizabeth. Come." He stood and backed up from Jim, motioning for his daughter. "This woman saved you?" He pointed at Mary.

"Yes pa-pa. And the man. They killed two Crazies who had tried to rape me." Hyde's face grew pale. He shot a glance at Jim. Suddenly, the sound of a woman's scream sounded from Harrod's cruiser. Another pirate sprinted from below, almost tripping over some of the other men as he weaved his way to the bridge.

"Captain Hyde!" he exclaimed, his hands shook as he clutched his rifle. "Captain Hyde! Cecilia is below in the infirmary. The medic was trying… he was…." The pirate pointed at Harrod.

"Shut your face private, Captain Hyde is dealing with an important matter!" Harrod snapped at the shaking man.

"No," the private said quietly.

"Excuse me?!" Harrod strode over to the man and unholstered his pistol.

"Harrod, let the man speak." Hyde stood and gently pushed Elizabeth behind one of his men.

"Captain!" the man exclaimed. Harrod pressed the muzzle of his pistol into the man's chest.

"He is disobeying my order's Captain, we will deal with this later." Harrod sneered and turned toward's Hyde.

"No, you are disobeying *MINE*. We will deal with all of this now." Hyde's voice thundered. Everyone on deck was silent.

"Harrod's wife was forced to have an abortion!" The private had mustered up just enough courage to yell every word. It was silent for several seconds after he spoke. Harrod clenched his teeth and turned back towards the man. Captain Hyde snapped his finger.

In one swift motion, his two lieutenants cut through the rope which fettered Jim and Mary while two other pirates rushed to restrain Harrod.

"Children," the Captain began, "are the lifeblood of our existence. *You*, Harrod, lied about these drifeters!" Hyde swiftly closed in towards Harrod as he spoke. "*You* tried to kill your wife's child! You endangered *MY DAUGHTER*!"

Harrod startled back, struggling against the men who restrained him. "I, she…"

"You know the penalty for lying; for murder!" Hyde exclaimed.

"I will not be exiled!" Harrod exclaimed. He then thrust his head forward, ramming one of the lieutenant's heads, knocking him unconscious. As the guard fell to the deck, Harrod grabbed his pistol and shot the other lieutenant in the face, then quickly turned, aiming at Hyde. He lined up the sights, pulling the trigger back. WHAM! Jim tackled Harrod, pinning him prone to the deck, digging his elbow into Harrod's head. The stray bullet zipped past Hyde.

"You're *DONE*!" Jim spat through clinched teeth.

"So you wanted to sell your own wife? And this man's *child*?" Mary stood up tall as spoke. Every man turned and was silent. The desert wind blew and caught Mary's hair. She strode slowly towards Harrod who struggled in vain against Jim's hold. "I risked everything to find my husband's DNA in an abandoned clinic, but I found it. I am now pregnant. You tried to abort your own child. You tried to have me raped and sold. You tried to have *her* raped and sold." Mary said, pointing to Elizabeth.

"Just…J-just let me go. I'll go and never come back!" Harrod struggled to speak as Jim pressed into his throat. "I g-get it. I'm exiled!"

"Exiled?" Captain Hyde stepped forward. "No! No, you'll be executed." Mary reached down for Harrod's black HK .45 which lay on the deck. Hyde nodded. Harrod struggled, looking up through the corner of his eye at her.

"So, you're gonna murder me, huh bitch?"

"No. This isn't murder. This is judgement. And *this* is mine now." Mary's lips moved firmly as she spoke, her thumb cocking the hammer and her finger pulling the trigger. *CRACK!!* Jim had tucked his head into his shoulder. Bits of flesh flew and dark blood pooled beneath Harrod's head, spreading across the hardwood. Jim shoved off of the lifeless chest as he stood. He looked at Mary. She stared at the pool of blood; it was dark like the sand.

VI

The sun began to creep over the dark pink and purple peaks of the sand dunes. Mary stood at the edge of the deck, wrapped in a blanket, with new tan boots covering her feet. Six lay next to Elizabeth a few feet away, licking her face as she giggled and hugged his neck. Captain Hyde smiled at his daughter. His eyes were relaxed now, soft, deep. He turned to Mary.

"I can't repay you." Hyde sighed.

"This is more than enough." Mary said, looking down at the black Land Rover parked on the sand.

"It's the least I could do," Hyde said. "You saved my Elizabeth. My life. Children are the future." Mary looked down and grinned.

"I know."

"There's plenty of water, whatever food we had to spare, and several AK-47s with 6 extra loaded mags. And you can keep that," Hyde nodded towards the pistol holstered at Mary's side. "The dead don't need it." Hyde turned as Jim approached, who had stopped briefly to rub Six's head.

"This is all I could find." Jim said, tossing Mary a black t-shirt.

"Metallica?" She looked up at him. "I do like the coiled snake." Jim turned as Mary dropped the blanket and slipped the black shirt on.

"Well, no one's gonna tread on you." Jim winked. "I know it's not Nirvana, but hey check out this Army jacket, it says Joseph!" Jim rolled his eyes.

"Well you'll always be Jim to me," Mary laughed. Captain Hyde walked over to his daughter ran his thick fingers through her red hair. Come on darling, time to say good bye. Elizabeth ran to Mary and hugged her waist, pressing her head into her stomach. Several tears formed in Mary's eyes as she embraced her. Each dripped down her cheek and fell into the girl's hair.

"Don't steal anymore cars, alright?" Jim grinned. Elizabeth let go of Mary and almost tackled Jim with her hug. "Hey! Alright, be good, kid." Elizabeth stepped back and blew Mary a kiss, who caught it and put it in her pocket. She took her father's hand and the two walked below deck.

"This should get us to the Badlands, right?" Mary asked.

"Should get us pretty far regardless." Jim nodded, looking down at their new ride.

"I'm glad you decided to come with me." Mary said.

"Well I didn't have anything better to do anyway." Jim grinned.

"And if anyone gets in our way, we'll fuck 'em up!"

"Hell, Mary!" Jim laughed. "Yeah, we will." Six jumped up and nudged Mary in the back of the knee. His dark brown hair and pointy ears rubbing against her pants.

"You too Six." Mary said rubbing his neck. She peered out at the dark sands. Still nearly black even in the light of the sun. She closed her eyes. A white dove rested on a large tree branch. A little boy played in a clear blue stream. Her eyes shot open. The sand was still black.

"You good?" Jim asked, nudging her arm.

"Yeah. Now let's blow this motherfucker."